The Mouse Bird

The Wish Fish Early Reader Series

by Heléna Macalino
Illustrated by: Milena Radeva

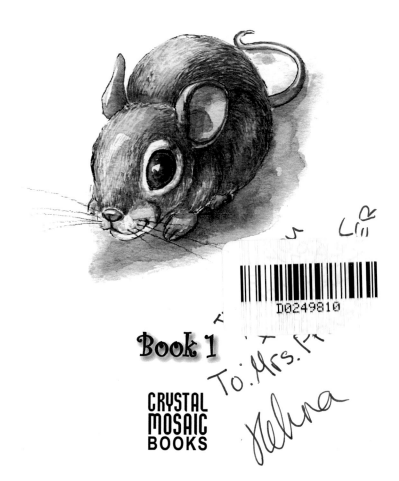

Book 1

CRYSTAL
MOSAIC
BOOKS

THE MOUSE BIRD
Text and layout by Heléna Macalino
Copyright© 2016
Illustrated by Milena Radeva

For information, address Crystal Mosaic Books,
PO Box 1276 Hillsboro, OR 97123
ISBN: 978-0-9911061-8-9

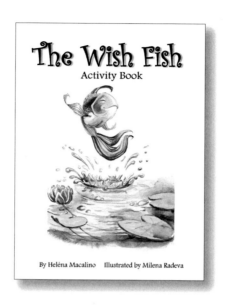

Get your free WISH FISH activity book
prepared especially for you by Heléna and Milena!
Go to www.macalino.com

DEDICATION PAGE
This book is dedicated to the memory of Cheese,
my hamster, the speediest runner in the world!

Come little children, I am the Wish Fish and I have a story to tell!

Intheshadiestwoodnearthegrassiest hills, in the coziest tree trunk near the sparkliest stream lived a mouse. This mouse had fur as brown as cocoa and eyes as black as the midnight sky. She had whiskers as clear as water pouring down from a waterfall and ears as round as acorns.

Her name was Squeak. Squeak always treated her neighbors kindly. She brought them cookies and made them leaf stem baskets for gathering seeds.

Squeak had a wonderful life. Except for one thing...

She was so very small.

And she didn't like that at all.

One day, Squeak scattered the leaves, looking for leftover seeds that the birds had dropped. Nearby, Hopper the Bunny hopped over the dirt beneath a fallen tree; Breeze the Blue Magpie flew through the branches of a great oak; and Chippy the Chipmunk scampered up the bark of an ancient redwood.

Squeak stood up on her hind legs and shouted, "Hey, you guys, come down! There's lots of sunflower seeds and corn kernels today."

Hopper hopped across to Squeak; Breeze glided down; and Chippy scurried over. They all dug under the leaves and helped Squeak look for seeds.

"Hey, you're right! There's a lot of seeds under here," Hopper said.

Breeze tried to brush the leaves aside with her wings, but they wouldn't move. "Squeak, can you come and help me uncover these seeds with your tiny paws?"

Squeak frowned. "Don't call me tiny, please."

Chippy stopped digging for seeds. "Why don't you like being small? You can do so many more things than we can."

"Yeah, like squeezing into teeny holes and exploring abandoned mouse houses under the roots," Hopper agreed.

Squeak put her paws on her hips. "Humph! Well, I just don't like being small! I can't..."

Hopper sat up straight; her ears perked and twitched.

"What's wrong?" asked Breeze.

"I heard a branch crack. Somebody's sneaking up on us," whispered Hopper.

The four friends froze. Hopper stared at her burrow; Breeze stared at her nest; Chippy stared at her hollow. And Squeak just stared.

"It's Mr. Fox!" Chippy cried, pointing to a familiar white-tipped orange tail in the bushes nearby.

"Run!" cawed Breeze.

Hopper dashed for her den where the fox could never dig her out; Breeze rocketed up to her nest where the fox could never climb to; Chippy boosted up the tree into her hole where the fox could never squeeze in.

And down in the leaves, Squeak crouched alone.

M

r. Fox pounced from out of the bushes. His paws landed on Squeak's tail.

She finally ran.

Squeak dashed through the hollow log like a bunny. Mr. Fox followed her right in.

Squeak rocketed down a fallen branch like a bird. Mr. Fox leaped down behind her.

Squeak boosted up a baby tree like a squirrel. Mr. Fox pushed the sapling right over.

Squeak squeaked in fright. Mr. Fox was going to eat her! She would never get to bake cookies again. She would never get to gather seeds with her friends again. She could not let that happen.

Squeak ran as fast as lightning over a patch of rocks.

Ahead she saw a fairly big rock with a teeny, teeny hole in it - just the size for a mouse. Squeak heard Mr. Fox's claws tapping against the rocks and the rocks clattering as they rolled away under his paws. Squeak heard Mr. Fox's growls as he sped toward her.

Squeak leaped. The wind ruffled her fur as she stretched her little body as thin as she could as she popped into the hole.

Mr. Fox jumped after her. She heard a big bonk!

The rock rolled. Squeak's whiskers quivered. With her tiny claws, she grasped at the walls of the hole. Outside the hole flashed grey rock, brown dirt, green trees, blue sky...and then grey rock, brown dirt, green trees, blue sky all over again.

Finally, the rock stopped rolling. Squeak saw the blue sky. A moment later, the hole went dark. A fuzzy paw and a sharp claw poked in, barely missing her nose.

Squeak was trapped!

Hours later Mr. Fox gave up.

Maybe. Or maybe Mr. Fox had just decided to sleep outside the rock the whole entire night until Squeak came out.

Squeak was terrified.

She squeezed back as far as she could into the hole and curled as tight as she could into the teensiest ball she could make, so Mr. Fox could not get her.

She went to sleep – and dreamed bad dreams.

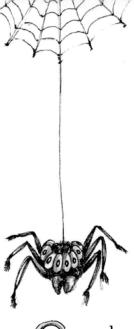

Squeak squirmed in her sleep. Something poked the side of her tummy. She flinched. Again, something poked her side even harder!

She woke up in fright.

Out of the opening to the rock hole, Squeak saw a long curved claw of a badger in the dark.

She squeaked!

The badger's sharp claw dug at Squeak's hiding rock. Would he ever leave? Finally, finally, she heard the clicking of rocks as the badger walked grumpily away.

Outside, the owl's hoot told Squeak that night had come. She couldn't see anything, not even the whiskers on her own nose.

Squeak squirmed. She turned and tossed. Then finally, she settled down and fell into her thoughts.

Why did I have to be born the smallest mouse?

If only I were bigger!

S queak twitched her whiskers. If you gathered the scents of the mint leaves, of the rose petals, and of the pine needles, mixed them in a pot, and threw them up into the air, then you would smell what Squeak smelled on that fresh morning.

Squeak opened her eyes. She saw the glitter like diamonds in the gray rock.

Quivering, she crept toward the mouth of her hole. She thought of her grandma's favorite saying, "Keep moving on!"

Squeak rocketed out of her hole and ran as fast as a cheetah all the way home.

Two days later, Squeak's neighbors knocked on her beautiful mouse hole door. Squeak had decorated her door with pinecones, swirls, and trees, and laid out a tidy welcome mat to make people feel good when they came to her doorstep, smelling her fresh baked cookies.

"Squeak, are you home? You haven't eaten for days! Would you like me to bring nuts?"

Squeak was too scared to answer. Squeak quivered with fear. She knew she had to eat something, but all she had left was an emergency basket of nuts and that would run out soon.

Squeak closed her eyes. She had a vision of flying as a bird and swooping down to get seeds without anyone seeing a glimpse of her brown eagle feathers.

Squeak flapped her arms; then she sighed.

"I wish I were bigger. Then I'd be safe."

S queak had an idea. She crept to her door and peeked out. Immediately, she slammed the door closed. She took a couple breaths. Those two breaths sailed into her body and built her courage. Slowly, Squeak opened the door again. She quietly and so, so, so slowly closed the door behind her and dashed to the house next door.

"Who is it?" asked a voice inside.

"It's Squeak! Hurry, hurry, let me in!"

The Mouse Witch opened the door and Squeak ran inside. Today, the Mouse Witch wore a black cloak with golden stars stitched into it like the twinkling stars of night. She already had her wand. She knew what Squeak had come for.

"You want to be bigger, don't you?" said the witch. "Well, that is a thing I cannot help you with, but I know someone who can."

"Oh, really!" said Squeak. "Who is it?! Who is it?!"

"Now, now, settle down. I will tell you how to find her. This is what you have to do. Listen very carefully: Find the stream with the sparkliest water. Follow it down to the tree with the mossiest trunk. There she will be waiting."

queak ran out of the house as soon as the Mouse Witch finished talking. Squeak ran so fast that she tumbled over her own paws right into Hopper the Bunny.

"Hopper! Do you know where to find the sparkliest stream?" Squeak asked.

"The other day I was hopping home and I saw a stream and thought it was a shame I didn't have time to play in it, it was so sparkly. I think it was by Breeze's nest out in the North Woods."

"Thanks!" said Squeak and dashed off toward the North Wood.

When she reached Breeze's nest, she looked around in a hurry. In a small, small clearing next to a couple of Spruce trees, something blue caught her eye. Squeak scurried over as fast as her legs would carry her.

The stream glimmered with sunlight. In a rush, Squeak bolted down the side of the stream and bumped into a mossy tree trunk older than her great-great-great grandfather.

Squeak almost fainted in relief. She had found it! The tree with the mossiest trunk!

S queak heard a voice. "Are you looking for me?" it said.

"Where are you? I can't see you," Squeak answered.

"Over here in the water."

Squeaked peered into the water. "All I see is a fish."

"I know, that's me: The Wish Fish," said the fish.

Squeak jumped back in fright. A talking fish?!

"Now what is your wish, little mouse?" the Wish Fish bubbled.

"I would like to be bigger," said Squeak firmly, stepping forward to get a better look at the fish. The fish leapt out of the water and Squeak gasped. The Wish Fish had gold and silver and blue scales. Her eyes shone blue as the sparkling water, and her tail held the colors of the rainbow.

"Very well then. Stand still or it might go wrong! Golden scale, silver scale, and blue.

Combine your power and make my friend's wish come true!"

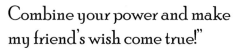

Poof!
A shower of gold, silver, and blue mist fell away.

In the center now, stood a huge, beautiful bird. Her wings and her body flashed silky  brown feathers. Her head was covered in silky brown mouse fur. Her perfect acorn-shaped ears twitched in the breeze along with her whiskers.

Squeak tested her wings. She felt them catch the wind.

"Thank you so much, Wish Fish!" Squeak shouted and swooped off into the beautiful blue sky.

Squeak stumbled as she landed, but she didn't care. She was just happy to be bigger! Around her stood tall birch trees. Purple windflowers and red tulips swayed in the breeze. Two springs bubbled on each side of the clearing.

A couple feet away Squeak saw two strange brown lumps sticking out of the side of a tree. Squeak took a few steps forward. The lumps jumped out at her. It was human feet!

"What an extraordinary bird! You have the body of a bird, the wings of a bird, but the head of a mouse! I must catch you!"

Squeak squeaked in fright. She leaped into the air and flapped her new wings hard just in time for the man's hand to brush her beautiful tail. The man plucked one silky brown feather from Squeak's poor tail.

Squeak glided down to the earth. Oh, how her little tail hurt!

In the quiet of the woods, Squeak heard a familiar thumping nearby. That sounded like Hopper! It was! She could see Hopper, Breeze, and Chippy gathering seeds for lunch. Squeak flew over to them.

"Hey guys! How are you doing? I missed you!"

Her three friends turned to see a huge bird with the head of a mouse. They all shrieked in horror.

"RUN FOR YOUR LIVES!" Hopper screamed.

Squeak's three friends vanished into the forest.

lowly, Squeak flew home. Her heart had a crack in it.

When Squeak landed in front of her home, she peered down at her tiny, beautiful door. Squeak realized she had a problem: she would not be able to go into her nice, teeny, comfortable house ever again.

Squeak heard a big grumble. It was her tummy. She turned to gather seeds, but even when she had pecked up a whole mouth full of seeds, it did not fill her tummy even a little bit.

Squeak hung her head in sadness.

S queak's sharp mouse ears twitched. She heard a human whispering. She listened harder.

"I told you that mouse bird was real!" he said.

Squeak's sharp mouse eyes found the man hiding behind a thick tree trunk. With him hid another man. The man had a net!

All of a sudden, the net came flying at her. Squeak ran. The net just barely missed her wing. It hit the ground. Immediately, the man threw another net at her.

Squeak realized that she was a bird now. She had wings! So she soared into the air as the net fell on the spot where she had stood.

Squeak flew over Breeze's nest and saw the sparkliest stream. She followed it down to the mossiest tree trunk. There she found the Wish Fish.

"Wish Fish, Wish Fish, come out!" she called.

She heard splashing in the water. Out popped the Wish Fish!

"Oh, Wish Fish! I'm so glad to see you! I came to tell you that I've learned my lesson. Everybody has problems no matter their size."

The Wish Fish said, "I am happy you learned your lesson. Now I will turn you back into a mouse. Remember, stand still or it might go wrong! Golden scale, silver scale, and blue. Combine your power and make my friend's wish come true!"

Poof!
A shower of gold, silver, and blue mist fell away.

In the center now stood a beautiful mouse. This mouse had fur as brown as cocoa and eyes as black as the midnight sky. She had whiskers as clear as water pouring down from a waterfall and ears as round as acorns.

Squeak loved how she looked! She was her real self again.

"Thank you so much. I will always remember you for this!" she said and scampered off back into the woods.

Squeak found her friends gathering seeds in a patch of sunlight shining through the trees. On a beautiful, tall redwood tree perched Chippy chatting with Breeze who sat on the branch next to her. Beside a purple violet, Hopper sat on the cool earth beneath the tree looking up at them.

"Hey guys! I'm here!" Squeak yelled.

Everyone turned to see her. They all ran toward her with so many questions: Where have you been? How are you? Are you okay?

Squeak just smiled. Squeak had a wonderful life. Especially one thing...

She was so very small.

And she liked that most of all.

ABOUT THE AUTHOR

Heléna Macalino loves to explore her dreams. She wanders along lovely garden paths with magical gates, finds her way into enchanted forests with animals who hide huge wishes in their hearts. And as a member of a family of writers, she records these adventures to share with fellow wanderers. Heléna wrote her first book when she was in 2nd grade, THE REFLECTION, an Alice in Wonderland style picture book about a little girl who falls through the reflection of a puddle. Now a 3rd grader, Heléna brings you her second book, THE MOUSE BIRD from her series THE WISH FISH.

Want to follow Heléna in her wanderings? When she's not cuddling with her cats or doodling in her drawing notebook, she can be found on her family's website:

www.macalino.com.

Subscribe to her newsletter on the website and be the first to know when the next edition of THE WISH FISH appears!

ABOUT THE ILLUSTRATOR

Milena Radeva is a dream-maker. She loves the magic of colours and their power to turn imagination into reality. Reality which every one of us can see, touch and feel in her children's books illustrations. Milena started drawing professionally when she was 12 years old, she studied in an Art high school, she has BA and MA in illustration and now she is working on her PhD. She has illustrated many children's books for authors from all around the world, and she is always looking for new book adventures, magical stories and cheerful characters. Because for her, every new book is a whole new world to be discovered.

If you are interested in Milena's artworks you can dive in her drawings by following her on facebook ~ MilenaRadevaArts or visit her website:

www.milena.seimenus.com

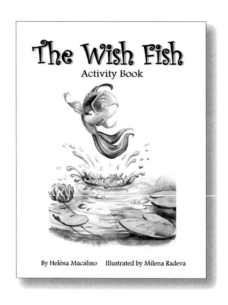

Get your free WISH FISH activity book
prepared especially for you by Heléna and Milena!
Go to www.macalino.com

COMING SOON

The second book in the WISH FISH SERIES:
THE CHIPMUNK KING

Wishes can be made in the woods!

Chippy the Chipmunk has a wonderful life,
bounding from tree to tree in the shady woods.

When an angry bear crashes into the friends'
campsite, Chippy's bossy habits keep Squeak,
Hopper, and Breeze from listening to his
warning. A frustrated Chippy doesn't realize
nobody knows everything all of the time.

Then he meets the Wish Fish...

Be careful what you wish for!

11307010R00031

Made in the USA
San Bernardino, CA
07 December 2018